A Note to Parents and Caregivers:

Read-it! Readers are for children who are just starting on the amazing road to reading. These beautiful books support both the acquisition of reading skills and the love of books.

The PURPLE LEVEL presents basic topics and objects using high frequency words and simple language patterns.

The RED LEVEL presents familiar topics using common words and repeating sentence patterns.

The BLUE LEVEL presents new ideas using a larger vocabulary and varied sentence structure.

The YELLOW LEVEL presents more challenging ideas, a broad vocabulary, and wide variety in sentence structure.

The GREEN LEVEL presents more complex ideas, an extended vocabulary range, and expanded language structures.

The ORANGE LEVEL presents a wide range of ideas and concepts using challenging vocabulary and complex language structures.

When sharing a book with your child, read in short stretches, pausing often to talk about the pictures. Have your child turn the pages and point to the pictures and familiar words. And be sure to reread favorite stories or parts of stories.

There is no right or wrong way to share books with children. Find time to read with your child, and pass on the legacy of literacy.

Adria F. Klein, Ph.D.
Professor Emeritus
California State University
San Bernardino, California

Editor: Jill Kalz
Page Production: Amy Bailey Muehlenhardt
Creative Director: Keith Griffin
Editorial Director: Carol Jones
Managing Editor: Catherine Neitge
The illustrations in this book were created with watercolor and colored pencil.

Picture Window Books
5115 Excelsior Boulevard
Suite 232
Minneapolis, MN 55416
877-845-8392
www.picturewindowbooks.com

Printed in the United States of America.

Library of Congress Cataloging-in-Publication Data
Jones, Christianne C.
Goldie's new home / by Christianne C. Jones ; illustrated by Amy Bailey
Muehlenhardt.
p. cm. — (Read-it! readers)
Summary: A little goldfish dreams of leaving the crowded pet store fish tank and
living in an aquarium of its own.
ISBN-10: 1-4048-1171-0 (hardcover)
[1. Goldfish—Fiction.] I. Muehlenhardt, Amy Bailey, 1974– ill. II. Title. III. Series.

PZ7.J6823Gol 2005
[E]—dc22   2005003857

Goldie's New Home

by Christianne C. Jones
illustrated by Amy Bailey Muehlenhardt

Special thanks to our advisers for their expertise:

Adria F. Klein, Ph.D.
Professor Emeritus, California State University
San Bernardino, California

Susan Kesselring, M.A.
Literacy Educator
Rosemount–Apple Valley–Eagan (Minnesota) School District

PICTURE WINDOW BOOKS
Minneapolis, Minnesota

Goldie lived in a pet store. She shared a tank with her best friends.

The tank was small and crowded.

Goldie liked her friends, but she wanted her own home.

Goldie wanted a big tank with lots of fresh water.

She wanted room to swim laps.

Goldie wanted her own castle, her own garden, and her own bubbling treasure chest.

Goldie wanted her own home.

Every time a customer came in the store, Goldie tried to get noticed.

She made cute faces. She danced.

She blew big, shiny bubbles.

But it wasn't easy to get noticed
with so many other fish around.

The net dipped into the water, but Goldie was never picked.

One day, Goldie was feeling extra sad. Customers came and went. Goldie didn't try to get noticed.

No cute faces. No dancing. No big, shiny bubbles. Goldie went to bed early.

Suddenly, she woke up. What was going on?

18

She was being scooped up in the net!

Goldie went to her new home.

She had her own tank, her own castle, her own garden, and her own bubbling treasure chest.

Goldie even had a new friend.

She loved her new home!

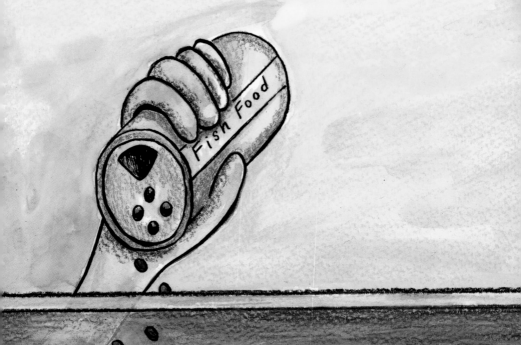

23

More *Read-it!* Readers

Bright pictures and fun stories help you practice your reading skills. Look for more books at your level.

Allie's Bike
The Bath
Busy Bear
Caleb's Race
Dad's Shirt
Danny's Birthday
Days of the Week
Fable's Whistle
Finny Learns to Swim
Jake Skates
New to Drew
The Princess and Her Pony
Riley Flies a Kite
The Tall, Tall Slide
The Traveling Shoes
Tricia's Talent
A Trip to the Zoo
Wendell the Worrier
Willy the Worm

Looking for a specific title or level? A complete list of *Read-it!* Readers is available on our Web site:
www.picturewindowbooks.com